★★★★ THE COBTOWN OBSERVER ★★★★

Christmas Eve, Wednesday, December 24, 1845. Weather: Snowy

TOWN NOTICES:

Mr. Edwin Hart tells us that Lucky's Spice Mill will be closed December 24 – 27 for an employee's holiday.

Heddy Peggler will be having a day of baking and wreath-making on Dec. 24.★

The General Store will be closed on Christmas Day, so get all your shopping done early! ★

Found: One black, brown, and white dog wearing a red collar and bell. Found by Jasper Payne. ★ ★

THAT'S WHAT THEY SAY!

The good children of Cobtown share their Christmas wishes:

★ I wish we could all have music on Christmas. —Lucky Hart

★ I wish that lost dog could find a good home.—Jasper Payne

★ I wish we could eat Christmas plum pudding every day!
—Valentine McGinty

★ I wish my Grandpa could be here with us instead of working in Ploomajiggy.
—Sissy Dingle

★ We wish we were taller so that our Christmas stockings would be bigger.
—The Ravenell Twins

★ We wish that Mr. Klingle could have a wonderful Christmas even though he is far from his home and family in the land of the Swiss.
—All of our children

COME ONE! COME ALL!
ON
CHRISTMAS DAY
TO
McGINTY'S
✶ MUSEUM ✶
FOR
MUSIC!
GAMES!
PANTOMIMES!
GHOST STORIES!
✶ MISTLETOE! ✶
HEAR the NEW
COBTOWN HYMN
SUNG BY
LUCKY HART
WITH WORDS BY
VIRGIL SQUIB.
REFRESHMENTS BY
✶ *PAYNE'S INN* ✶

FOR CHRISTMAS!
ORANGES!
ORANGES!
ORANGES!
And for your baking needs:
Fine Flour, Dried and Candied Fruits, Nuts, Sugar Cones, Yeast and
a complete selection of
Lucky's Spices.
And for good Children:

And for the Courting:
MISTLETOE!
And a fine assortment of
Hats, Bonnets, Shoes, Gloves, Ribbons, Pins, Lace, Yard Goods, Etc.
IF YOU WANT IT, WE HAVE GOT IT!
at the
GENERAL STORE.

✶ ✶ ✶ ✶

✶None Better!✶

✶ ✶ ✶ ✶

A VERY MERRY
✶CHRISTMAS✶
from all of us at
Payne's Inn & Tavern.
In the heart of Cobtown.

THE STRANGER

A COBTOWN Christmas

From the Diaries of
Lucky Hart

Written by
JULIA VAN NUTT
Illustrated by
ROBERT VAN NUTT

A Doubleday Book for Young Readers

VIRGIL SQUIB

For all who make music and thus bring MAGIC into the world.
J.V.N.

For my mother, who believed, not only in Cobtown, but in us.
R.V.N.

A DOUBLEDAY BOOK FOR YOUNG READERS
Published by Bantam Doubleday Dell Publishing Group, Inc.
1540 Broadway
New York, New York 10036
Doubleday and the portrayal of an anchor with a dolphin are trademarks of
Bantam Doubleday Dell Publishing Group, Inc.

Cataloging-in-Publication Data is available from the Library of Congress.
ISBN 0-385-32556-8

The text of this book is set in 15-point Greg.
Book design by Robert Van Nutt

Manufactured in the United States of America
November 1998
10 9 8 7 6 5 4 3 2 1

In Grandma's Kitchen

"If you see anything in there you want, go ahead and take it," Grandma said. We were helping to clean out her old kitchen cabinets. We were surrounded by oversized cooking pots and big old wooden spoons, things that spoke of a time when the family was larger and there were more mouths to feed. I gathered some of the smaller items to take away with me.

A final glance into an apparently empty cupboard revealed a small dark jar and a little book pushed back in the corner. I gently opened the red leather-bound book. It was full of recipes, all carefully written down in a neat hand. On the cover was a label inscribed: "For my Mother, Cinnamon Hart, Christmas, 1845, from her Loving Daughter, Lucky."

"Who are Cinnamon and Lucky, Grandma?" I asked.

"Lucky was my grandmother, honey," she answered. "Cinnamon Hart was her mother. Lucky was quite a writer. There's a trunk full of her old notebooks and such up in the attic. If you feel like going up there and looking around, you may find them."

I took my treasures up to the attic and began my search. Sure enough, I found the trunk and could hardly believe all that it held. Lucky had written diaries all through her childhood and had saved these along with newspapers and posters and all sorts of other things. I looked through the diaries and found the one for Christmas, 1845. I had almost forgotten the little jar that I had found in the cupboard. It had a label that read LUCKY'S KITCHEN PEPPER, and there was still something inside. When I opened it and sniffed, the most wonderful smell of spices filled the air. It was the smell of the Christmas of 1845, and this is its story as written in the diary of Lucky Hart.

THE
TOWN HYMN.

DECEMBER 21, 1845

Christmas is just days away! There is lots of excitement here in Cobtown. I am busy making presents and trying to memorize the words to a new song. I have to sing it for the whole town on Christmas Day! It's called the Cobtown Hymn. It was written by our town poet, Virgil Squib. He's also the station master for the rail-road.

The McGinty family, who live at the top of the hill and run McGinty's Museum, have the only musical instrument in town. They always hold a Christmas Day Party. That's when I will sing the Cobtown Hymn. Minerva Mackadoo McGinty will accompany me on her pump organ. Folks tell me that I am blessed to have such a clear singing voice, but there are other things I'd rather do than memorize the new Hymn.

A LIST OF THINGS
I'D RATHER BE DOING:

1. Eating Christmas cookies.
2. Making a snowman with my friends (if there was any snow).
3. Eating Christmas plum pudding.
4. Making Pomanders.
5. Ice skating.
6. Making Mama's Christmas gift.
7. Baking more Christmas cookies. (I ate all the first ones!)
8. Decorating Fliberty's for the Animals' Christmas Eve Party.
9. Making Christmas wreaths.
10. Drinking hot spiced cider.

So far, Mama and I have made a new lace bonnet for dear Aunt Heddy Peggler. I have knitted a golden yellow muffler for my father. My mother's present will be a cooking book that I shall fill with her best recipes. It is not finished because the red notebook I ordered has yet to arrive by train. I keep going down to the station to see if the book is here yet. So far, no luck.

Dear old Fliberty Jibbert meets every train in case something arrives for our mills. He has worked for our family for over fifty years and is practically kin. I have knitted him a bright blue muffler for Christmas.

"Of course, I'm making dog soup! It wouldn't be Christmas without it!" Fliberty told me this morning as I rode over to the station with him. He means he will be cooking soup for the dogs to eat. It's part of the yearly Animals' Christmas Eve Party that we all attend at his place. Everybody in town brings their animals. I asked him how he makes dog soup. He says it is different every year but he wrote down most of the things that go into it. Maybe I will write it into Mama's new cooking book.

DOG SOUP – BY FLIBERTY J.

1- ASK EVERYBODY TO SAVE THEIR BONES-ALL KINDS.
2- COVER THEM BONES WITH WATER AND BOIL THEM.
3. ADD ANY LEFTOVERS-INCLUDING GRISTLE, DISGUSTING CRITTER PARTS AND VEGETABLES.
4. COOK IT FOR 3 HOURS, THEN ADD OLD BREAD.
5. CALL THE DOGS AND STAND BACK!

COBTOWN

Virgil Squib, the station master, tells me I don't have to keep coming down there to check on that notebook, but I can't help it. Anyhow, it's exciting at the station. Old Hans Van Ripper and his goat, Buckeye, meet every train too, as there is always something for them to cart up to Ravenell's General Store. Jasper Payne is there to direct guests to his family's Inn, and Valentine McGinty is usually passing out handbills for McGinty's Museum.

Since I was at the station, Virgil Squib asked me to sing his Cobtown Hymn, just to make sure I'm learning the words exactly the way he wrote them.

"Virgil, I've got other things to think about right now," I wanted to tell him, but I just stuck my head into the ticket window and sang real loud, hoping he'd get enough of that song for the time being.

After all of that, the notebook for Mama's present still did not arrive. I will go again tomorrow.

No. 179

THE COBTOWN GENERAL STORE.
• JOSIAH RAVENELL, PROPRIETOR. •
"IF YOU WANT IT, WE HAVE GOT IT!"

Date: Dec 15, 1845

Description of goods:	Price:
One notebook with red striped cover, red leather spine and corners... —To be ordered from Ploomajiggy and shipped by Rail-road. Received from Miss L. Hart 35¢ cash. J. Ravenell.	35¢ Paid in full 12/15/45

CORTOWN

DECEMBER 22, 1845

I'm glad that I was over at the station today because Cobtown got a surprise when the train pulled in. There, on board, was a mysterious blind man who does not speak English but some other tongue that sounds like pure gibberish. He didn't have a train ticket, in fact he didn't even want to ride the train. The train crew had to force him on board.

According to the engineer, they spotted the stranger stumbling around in Dizzard. That is where the train stops to take on water. Nothing is there but lots of dead weeds and some icy puddles. They found him all alone and blind and obviously lost and unable to tell them anything. So, they decided to bring him here to Cobtown, at least for tonight.

They say he kept on hollerin', "Jingle, jingle!" Then as they pushed him onto the train, he pushed back, shaking his head and saying, "Nine donkeys." Then he kept saying something about a "hair vinkle." Nobody knows what it all means, if indeed it means anything.

Here's what we decided. If there's anybody around here who knows all about donkeys, it's Fliberty Jibbert. "Let's take him down to my place to spend the night. I know he keeps talking about 'nine donkeys,' and I've only got three, but that will just have to do for now," Fliberty said. "I don't know what a 'hair vinkle' is, but maybe they have one at Ravenell's General Store. After all, their motto is 'If you want it, we have got it!'"

The blind stranger rode back to the mills with Fliberty and me. I must say that he looked confused. I am sure he does not know where he is. He just held on tightly to the seat. Once I saw him rub his face and stare up to the sky and whisper, "Jingle, jingle." Then his eyes got all full of tears. I touched his hand and he grabbed my hand and squeezed it. I think he knows we mean to look after him.

If my father, Edwin Hart, whose family has sailed the seven seas, was here, he would know where this stranger comes from. Mama says Papa will be home by Christmas.

Maybe Mama's notebook will come tomorrow. I do so hope, hope, hope that it will!!!

Two of Papa's old tickets.

McGINTY'S
MUSEUM

McGINTY'S MUSEUM
GENERAL STORE
READ
THE CORTOWN OBSERVER
CORTOWN

December 23, 1845

Last night as I slept, a band of Christmas angels passed by, leaving behind a beautiful white blanket. The blanket covers all of Cobtown and is made of snow. Christmas just got even better. I ate snow cream for breakfast.

Today, Mama, Aunt Heddy and I baked lots of cookies and pies and cakes. We made spice cookies using Lucky's Kitchen Pepper. It is made from a secret formula that only my father knows. It has cinnamon and cloves in it, but I do not know what else. I baked extra cookies for the blind man.

My hands still smell real good from making the pomanders. We tied the ribbons on them at Aunt Heddy's. Now they are ready to give as Christmas gifts. Everybody likes to get them because it makes their room smell good all winter.

How to make Pomanders

1. Get an apple (not too big).
2. Get whole cloves (lots!)
3. Stick cloves into the apple. Try not to break their heads.
4. Wait a week as it shrinks.

Then, tie it with a ribbon.

Late this afternoon, we went up to the McGintys' to practice our Christmas carols. Well, right in the middle of a good song, the pump organ hissed and went silent. When Mrs. McGinty pumped the pedals we could hear it breathe but no music came out. As usual, we all turned to Fliberty, who can fix everything.

"Oh, I can fix it, but not by Christmas," he told us.

Christmas without music? What a dismal thought!

In all the excitement, I forgot to ask about Mama's notebook arriving. It did. Mr. Ravenell at the General Store sent Old Hans and Buckeye over with it after I got back home. I have hidden it from Mama so she will be surprised on Christmas. Now I must stop writing this and begin putting in as many recipes as I can before bedtime. The recipe for snow cream will be first.

Aunt Heddy gave me this.

Snow Cream

For Lucky, from her Aunt Heddy, Dec. 1845

Put out a pan when it begins to snow. Be sure it is where the animals can't walk in it. When it is full, mix in:

1 Teaspoon of vanilla
2 cups of sugar
2 cups of cream

and a pinch of Lucky's Kitchen Pepper.

Mix it all thoroughly and eat it at once.

Be sure to use only clean snow!

THE
COBTOWN HYMN
1845

Christmas Eve–We have just finished supper and I have time to write this before we go to the Animals' Christmas Eve Party. Today Papa returned from his business trip. I am so glad he is back home. I completed Mama's cooking book this morning and then went up to Aunt Heddy's. While we were there, making wreaths for Fliberty's party, Jasper came running up to her door. He was out of breath and excited. "I just found a sick dog. Can I bring him here for you to doctor?"

Aunt Heddy knows all about doctoring folks and animals.

"Of course you can bring him over," she told him.

Aunt Heddy's little wild pig, Oinkey, lives there with her and he is as good a pig as you would ever want to know. She has given him his own dish and rug by the fire. He is very jealous of his rug and whenever another animal tries to lie on it, Oinkey will push him off with his snout.

So, while we were waiting for the sick dog to arrive, Heddy said, "I better fix him his own bedding by the fire. Oinkey won't give his up for anybody, even on Christmas Eve."

As we were preparing a spot for the sick dog, Jasper returned with the dog, who seems well fed and who wears a bell around his neck. He limps as if his feet hurt from walking too much. He looked around the room and limped right over to Oinkey's bed and lay down.

Oinkey the wild pig

None of us could believe it when we saw Oinkey sniff the new dog, then just lie down next to him, like they were the best friends on earth.

"Maybe Oinkey does have the Christmas spirit of giving, Aunt Heddy," I told her.

Aunt Heddy washed the dog's paws and oiled them. We rubbed him good and fed him. He slept by the fire all day and rested his head on Oinkey like a pillow.

When we finished our garlands and wreaths, we took them and our ice skates down to Fliberty's.

The blind man is still staying down there. Papa spent a lot of time with him and discovered some things. His name is Fritz Klingle and he is from a land called Swiss. Turns out, he doesn't speak gibberish. "Nine donkeys" is the way that Mr. Klingle says "No, thank you" in the language of the Swiss. There was a notice in the newspaper about a missing blind man. It is Mr. Klingle. The notice asks anyone with information to contact a Mr. Winkle. Father says that is the "hair vinkle" that Mr. Klingle was talking about. "Hair" is how they say "Mister" in Swiss. Father has written to this Hair Winkle.

We had a good time hanging up the garlands and the wreaths at Fliberty's. Mr. Klingle sat by the fire as we worked. I made sure he got some of my Christmas cookies. He seemed to enjoy sniffing them as much as eating them. I have decided to give him a bottle of Kitchen Pepper for a Christmas present. That way, whenever he smells it, he will think of his friends here in Cobtown.

Oinkey started behaving in an unusual way. He had never crossed paths with Mr. Klingle until he got down to Fliberty's with us. As soon as Oinkey got near him, he started sniffing the blind man. Then, Oinkey seemed to get excited. He started pushing Mr. Klingle with his snout, pretty hard, too. He tried to push him right out into the snow! None of us ever saw Oinkey be anything but polite, until now.

"Hey, Oinkey, stop it! Leave Mr. Klingle alone! What's got into that pig today?" Jasper asked.

As we were decorating, Valentine asked me if I was still learning the Cobtown Hymn. "I've learned all of the words but now that there will be no music, I don't expect to be able to sing it for everybody," I told him.

"Can't you sing it without somebody playing along?" Sissy Dingle asked. "Why don't you try it, just for us?"

So I tried it and I got through both verses but I felt nervous to do it alone. Besides, it just wasn't as good without music.

"You've got this place looking beautiful," Fliberty told us. "Now, I have a little Christmas surprise for you." He pushed something large and covered with a blanket across the snow and out onto the frozen pond. With a little flourish, Fliberty pulled off the cover to reveal a chair built right onto ice skates.

"You and Oinkey must be the first," he told Aunt Heddy, as he helped her up onto the ice throne.

We skated right behind them and never had more fun. As we made another turn around the pond, Jasper said, "Look at Mr. Klingle, he seems lonesome over there by himself."

Mr. Klingle must have heard his name because he lifted his head. Then he started out towards us, using his stick to feel his way. Valentine took him by the hand and led him to the ice chair.

Fliberty helped Aunt Heddy down and then took Mr. Klingle's arm and got him seated. As they took off across the ice Mr. Klingle's face lit up in the prettiest smile we had ever seen. We took turns pushing him around and around until suppertime.

I must leave off writing now, because the Animals' Christmas Eve Party is about to start!

Starting today, **Christmas Day, 1845,** I officially proclaim that I, Lucky Hart, do truly believe in Christmas miracles!

Lucky Hart, her mark.

Last night, at the Animals' Christmas Eve Party, Old Hans and his goat, Buckeye, were the first to show up. Shadrack and Meshack, Sissy's brothers, brought their ox, Tiny Albert. Fliberty had his donkeys, Muddy, Buddy and Sid, all brushed and clean. The McGintys brought Peale, their family dog. Aunt Heddy had Oinkey wearing a green ribbon and smelling like a pine forest.

Jasper said to Aunt Heddy, "Everybody's here except the sick dog. I'll go up and get him with my sled."

"I'll come, too," I said. "Me, too!" said all of the other children. We hurried back up to Aunt Heddy's with Oinkey. We put the dog into the sled and as we came back down the hill, he stood up, as if he was having fun. The bell he wore around his neck jingled as he looked this way and that.

Night was beginning to fall as we approached Fliberty's. Within we could see all of our beloved friends and animals, lit by the golden firelight. Then we saw Mr. Klingle stand up. He put his hands out in front of him as he headed in our direction, and started shouting, "Jingle! Jingle! JINGLE!" At the same time, the stray dog jumped down off the sled and started running right towards Fritz Klingle. He was wagging his tail and jumping up and down as if his feet didn't hurt him anymore.

"Do they know each other?" Jasper asked.

The "Jingle" talk from Mr. Klingle was just the way he calls his dog. That is the dog's name, Jingle. They had become separated on the day that the train people found him. Mr. Klingle didn't want to leave that spot because Jingle was somewhere nearby. Somehow Jingle made his way to Cobtown, where Mr. Klingle was taken. How could Jingle know where to go? That's part of the Christmas miracle, but here's something else.

We all went back into Fliberty's and gathered around the fire. Mr. Klingle got down on the floor next to Jingle and cried tears of joy. Then he smiled and said, in real clear English, "The Merry Christmas, yah."

Oinkey went over to where Mr. Klingle was hugging Jingle and gave him another shove with his snout. Next thing you know, Oinkey had squeezed right in between the two, like the filling of a sandwich, and started squealing. That made everybody laugh.

Did Oinkey know these two belonged together right from the first time he saw Mr. Klingle? Was that why he was trying to push him outside into the snow yesterday? Would he have pushed him all the way up the hill to Aunt Heddy's, where Jingle slept in Oinkey's own bed? We will never know for sure.

Mr. Klingle stood up and opened his knapsack. The light of the fire made the inside of the sack glow with a golden light as he lifted out eight shining bells and placed them in a row before him. We all grew silent. He turned to me and said, "Lucky?"

As he picked up the bells, one by one, he played, most perfectly, the Cobtown Hymn. His bells chimed with a purity that took away my breath. I was so surprised that at first I could only listen. But as he played it through a second time, I joined in, singing the best I ever did sing. The Hymn never sounded so beautiful.

After only a short pause, he burst loose with JOY TO THE WORLD. His bells rang with the sweetest sound we had ever heard. And as we listened, we started to sing along. We knew that Fritz Klingle had given Cobtown the best Christmas gift of all.

THAT'S WHAT THEY SAY!

The good children of Cobtown share their Christmas wishes:

★ I wish we could all have music on Christmas. —Lucky Hart

★ I wish that lost dog could find a good home.—Jasper Payne

Some Christmas wishes do come true!

THE COBTOWN HYMN.

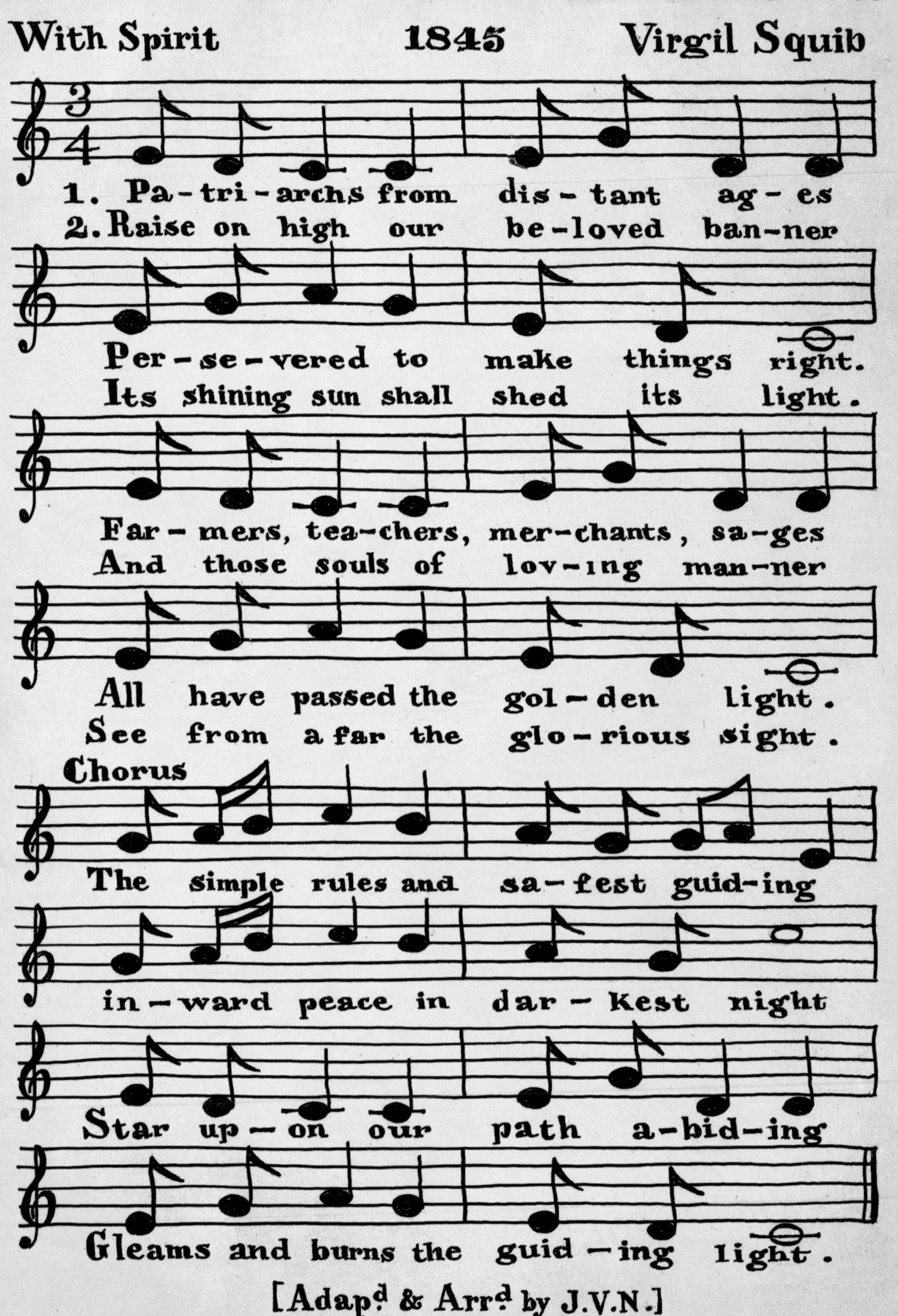

THE COBTOWN OBSERVER

I.B. HOOTIE: CHIEF CORRESPONDENT, EDITOR, PRINTER AND PUBLISHER.

CHRISTMAS IN COBTOWN

Once again the Season of Joy is upon us and good cheer abounds as Cobtown prepares for Christmas. Josiah and Mary Ravenell at the General Store report a busy trade in flour, sugar loaves, nuts and Lucky's Spices. Looks like a whole lot of baking going on. Mrs. Ravenell says ribbons are going fast, so get 'em while they last.

Fliberty Jibbert will hold his delightful Animals' Christmas Eve Party as usual. All are invited whether they bring an animal or not.

McGinty's Museum is planning a festive Christmas Day Party of music, games and entertainment. Hans Van Ripper will tell a ghost story, and we can look forward to poetic recitations by Vashti McGinty and Virgil Squib.

Payne's Inn has had to take on more help. They are needed in the kitchen to cope with the demand for extra pies and cakes for McGinty's party.

A MUSICAL DISASTER!

We have tragic news from McGinty's. The pump organ that was to provide the musical entertainment for the Christmas Party has broken down. "It only wheezes sadly now and will not give forth its rich and vibrant notes" said Minerva Mackadoo McGinty. "Alas, it will take days to fix." This must be especially bad news to Virgil Squib, Cobtown's Poet Laureate and station master, as he has just composed a "Cobtown Hymn" for Christmas. The hymn was to have its premiere performance at the McGinty's party. Young Lucky Hart was to have sung it to the accompaniment of the [now defunct] pump organ.

The town's only other musician, Jeramiah Dingle, will be away [in Ploomajiggy] with his fiddle on Christmas because of a prior agreement.

STRANGER LOST & FOUND

We have received a letter, a copy of which was sent to all the newspapers hereabouts, asking for news of a missing blind man. His name is Fritz Klingle and he is a member of Mr.Hermann Winkle's touring company of Swiss entertainers. He states that Mr.Klingle was visiting a distant relation, living near Dizzard, when he disappeared. "With the Wagon I come to get him," Mr.Winkle writes, "at the place where the Road meets the Railway, but there, he was not! He is lost in this Vast and Wild America!"

Well, we are happy to report that Mr.Klingle has been found. The crew of the morning train from Ploomajiggy found him alone and apparently lost. As it looked like it was about to snow, they brought him along to Cobtown. Mr.Edwin Hart interviewed the man and confirm that he is the missing Swiss. It looks like Mr. Klingle will be with us for Christmas.